This book belongs to

Aubree wilson -R

THE EMPEROR'S NEW CLOTHES

Adapted by Mary Packard from the original
TIMELESS TALES FROM HALLMARK™ story

BedrockPress™

Atlanta

Once upon a time, in the land of Oaf, there lived an emperor who loved clothes—the more expensive, the better.

The citizens of Oaf paid high taxes to keep their emperor dressed in the latest fashions. But because the land of Oaf was such a thriving place, without sickness, hunger, or war, they didn't mind the high taxes. They even joked how the emperor would never fight in a war for fear he would dirty his clothes.

Unfortunately, an evil plot was being hatched nearby.

The people of Rancor Island were planning to invade the land of Oaf, and for a bag of gold, the emperor's own minister, Sir Slippery, was going to help them.

One day, as the vain emperor was admiring himself in the mirror, Sir Slippery stole some top-secret papers from the emperor's robe. He wasted no time in handing these important documents over to the leaders of the Rancor Islanders.

"My emperor is a fool," Sir Slippery told them. "He was so busy listening to me tell him how wonderful he looked that he never even noticed when I picked his pocket."

Sir Slippery didn't know it, but two swindlers, Sylvester and Arthur, were watching and listening from a cliff high above.

"Did you hear that, Artie?" asked Sylvester. "This emperor must be the vainest emperor of all time. I bet if we put our heads together we could cheat him out of a fortune."

"No doubt about it, Sly," replied Arthur.

Soon the two sidekicks had come up with the perfect plan.

Meanwhile, the emperor was having a miserable day. Matilda, his wardrobe mistress, had brought him several racks of new clothes, and he hated every one of them.

"That robe is not purple enough!" bellowed the emperor, as Matilda showed him a rich, fur-trimmed coat. "And that one is too long!" he said, as she showed him another. "And that one's too short!" he said about a third.

"What do you think, Sir Buffoon?" he asked his trusted minister.

"You're absolutely right, Your Majesty," Sir Buffoon replied, too afraid of the emperor to say what he really thought.

The emperor did not like any of the clothes Matilda had made.

"Humph!" Matilda muttered under her breath. "There's nothing wrong with these clothes that a new emperor wouldn't fix!"

When the emperor had finished trying on the clothes, he demanded to see more by the following day.

"Tomorrow!" cried Matilda. "That's not nearly enough time!"

Just at that moment, one of the emperor's pages appeared.

"Two weavers have come a great distance to see you, Your Highness," said the page.

"Send them in immediately," the emperor ordered.

"Presenting Sylvester and Arthur, weavers to the crowned heads of the world," announced the page.

"But you can call us Sly and Artie, Your Majesty," said Sly. "Your reputation for good taste is known far and wide," he added.

The emperor was flattered by this praise. "How may I help you?" he asked.

"No, Your Majesty," said Sly. "It's how *we* may help *you*." He began measuring the emperor, all the while bragging about his famous customers. "Naturally, only someone with exquisite taste can see the beauty and workmanship in our clothes," he added. "Fools, and those not loyal to the emperor, cannot see anything at all."

"And you—the highest of the high-born—will certainly be able to appreciate the variety of purples woven into the fabric and the 24-karat gold thread we use to stitch the intricate designs," continued Sly.

"I will? I mean, of course I will!" said the vain emperor. "I command you to begin work at once."

"You don't really believe these phonies, do you?" Matilda asked indignantly.

"Don't be so jealous, Matilda," the emperor said. "I'm very interested in seeing what these weavers can do."

"Of course, we'll need plenty of money to buy materials," Sly said. "Fabric made of gold fibers doesn't come cheap."

"Money won't be a problem," replied the emperor, "but how soon will you be finished?"

"I can't tell yet," said Sly, "but you and anyone else are welcome to come and watch us work."

"Yes, come and see us anytime," added Artie.

Sly and Artie set up shop. They bought a huge loom and pretended to weave, although not one single thread was placed upon the loom.

It wasn't long before everyone in the land of Oaf heard about the emperor's new weavers and how only fools, or those disloyal to the emperor, could not appreciate their amazing work. All day long, people came to watch. Since they didn't want to seem foolish, they raved on and on about the marvelous material and the beautiful colors—even though there was nothing there to see.

"Ooooo! I've never seen anything like it!" exclaimed one of the townspeople.

"Such amazing designs!" cried another.

Sly and Artie tried to hide their laughter, but they couldn't help smiling when they thought of all the money they were going to make.

Meanwhile, all the emperor could think about were his new clothes.

"Why don't you go and have a look?" suggested Matilda. "Certainly you're not worried about appearing foolish, are you?"

"Of course not," said the emperor. But really he was worried, so he sent Sir Buffoon instead.

Sir Buffoon arrived at the weavers' workshop and stood before the loom.

"I don't see a thing," he mumbled to himself. "I know I'm loyal to the emperor. Is it possible I'm a fool?"

"What's the matter?" asked Sly. "Can't you see the beautiful shades of purple woven into the fabric?"

"Oh, yes, of course," Sir Buffoon quickly answered. "Um, maybe that shade of purple is a little off."

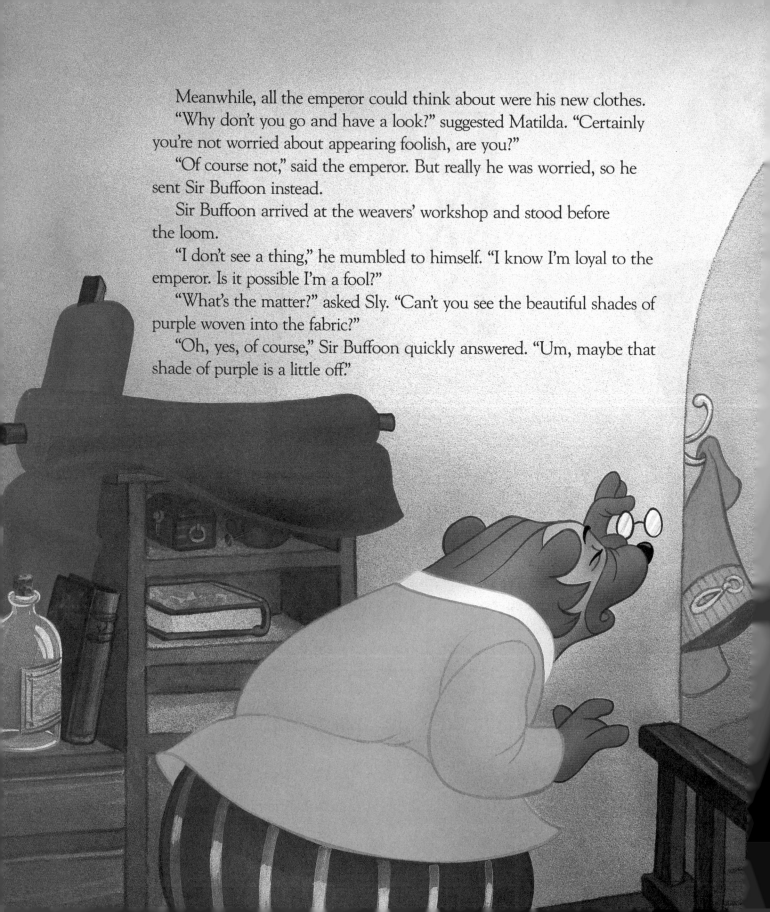

"It'll be fixed right away," Sly promised. Then he said, "Perhaps I should point out some of the best patterns. Just so you can describe them to the emperor."

"Oh, yes, thank you," said Sir Buffoon. And he listened very carefully so that he could repeat everything he heard.

When he returned to the palace, Sir Buffoon told the emperor all about his amazing new clothes.

"There are many lovely purples and lots of silver and gold," he explained. "You will absolutely glitter!"

The emperor clapped his hands with glee. "Tell me again!" he commanded.

"But Your Majesty," protested Sir Buffoon, "I've already told you seventeen times!"

The king finally allowed Sir Buffoon to leave, but not before making him describe the clothes one last time. Then he called for Sir Slippery.

"I want to show off my new clothes! See to it that I have a parade!"

"Yes, Your Highness," said Sir Slippery. But just as soon as Sir Slippery had finished planning the parade, he ran off to tell the Rancor Islanders about it.

"The emperor will be marching through the streets of the city all day on Sunday. It will be the perfect time for an invasion. Everyone will be watching the parade—no one will be prepared to fight."

On Sunday morning, Sly and Artie arrived at the castle with the emperor's new clothes.

The emperor looked hard, but try as he might, he could see nothing. But he refused to admit this because he didn't want to be thought a fool.

"This material is lighter than a spider's web," said Sly, as he slipped the imaginary robe over the emperor's head, "so it may feel like you're wearing nothing at all."

"Quite right," replied the emperor. "It feels as light as a feather. But how do I look?"

"You look marvelous!" exclaimed Sly.

So the emperor marched proudly through the castle door wearing nothing but his underwear.

Soon he was strutting down the avenues of Oaf, smiling kindly at all the people who had come to see his wonderful new clothes. The citizens of Oaf didn't want to look like fools, so they pretended they could see the clothes. They pretended so hard that they began to believe they really could see them.

"Look at the emperor's new clothes!" shouted a citizen. "They're even more wonderful than I'd heard."

Everyone cheered as the emperor passed, and the emperor felt better than he had in all his life.

Suddenly a little boy pointed his finger at the emperor and asked, "Why isn't the emperor wearing any clothes?"

The crowd gasped. Their emperor without clothes? Then they took a second look.

"I don't see any new clothes, either!" cried another parade watcher.

One by one, the citizens of Oaf began to laugh. They couldn't stop themselves—not even when the Rancor Islanders had them surrounded.

"You will surrender—immediately!" commanded the leader of the invading army.

But the citizens of Oaf just kept laughing until their insides ached and tears streamed down their faces.

"I demand to know what is so funny!" said the angry leader.

"Look at the emperor," they replied. "He hasn't any clothes on!"

The leader took one look at the emperor and burst out laughing, as did all his soldiers.

"Everyone is laughing at me!" cried the emperor.

"Yes," replied Matilda, "but at least you've saved the kingdom."

"I have? How?" asked the emperor.

"You looked so ridiculous that we couldn't help laughing. And our laughter caused the invaders to laugh," she answered. "It's hard to fight a battle when everyone is having such as good time, so they retreated. You're a hero!"

"I am? Oh, I am!" agreed the emperor happily.

"Hip, hip, hooray!" cried his subjects.

From that day on, the emperor and Matilda made all of his wardrobe decisions together—as husband and wife!
And everyone in Oaf lived happily ever after.

Published by Bedrock Press, an imprint of Turner Publishing, Inc.
A Subsidiary of Turner Broadcasting System, Inc.
1050 Techwood Drive, N.W. • Atlanta, Georgia 30318

Printed in Canada
First Edition 10 9 8 7 6 5 4 3 2 1
ISBN 1-57036-006-5

Designed by Antler & Baldwin Design Group • Developed by Nancy Hall, Inc.
Illustrations by Vaccaro Associates, Inc. • Painted by Eric Binder

Herodotus wrote that the Scythians who looted the temple of Aphrodite Urania in Ashkelon were damned with a 'female illness' by the aforementioned goddess,[1] and from this point on some Scythians who were born male felt a feminine soul inside of them and wore feminine clothing – long dresses with capes, furs or hemp fibres. This constitutes the first 'scientific' study of transness in world history.

Describing the customs of the Scythians, Herodotus noted the high social status of the Enarei, who performed sacred functions, practising divination on vines or linden bark. This process is similar to Chinese divination, as made famous by *The Book of Changes* (*I Ching*). The bark or twig was cut into three parts, after which the length of the sticks determined the divination that was made. Whenever Scythian kings fell ill, they would call upon the Enarei to determine which opponent had bewitched them.[2] The Enarei worshipped Artimpasa, the Scythian goddess of love and starry skies, and the priests of this goddess came from their order.

In fact, in many cultures around the world, trans people were historically regarded as being gifted with sacred abilities by some higher power. The Scythians' western neighbours were the Thracians, who lived not only in the eastern Balkans, but also in present-day Zakarpatia and Odesa. To honour Kotys, the Thracian goddess of vegetation and fertility, priests clad in feminine clothing would perform sacred orgiastic rites.[3] As time went by, the cult of Kotys spread to the Greeks as well, and the name Kotys was taken by some Thracian and Greek (in the Crimea) kings.

---

1 Herodotus, *Book I: Cleo, Histories*.

2 Herodotus, *Book IV: Melpomene, Histories*.

3 See Hans Licht, *Sexual Life in Ancient Greece*. See first footnote to p. 30.

On the eastern outskirts of the Indo-European linguistic and ethnocultural community, particularly in India (a country of 'blessed Rahmans', according to Ukrainian mythology), transgender people were referred to as hijras.

According to one myth, when Rama (a prince, one of the earthly incarnations of the Indo-Aryan supreme deity Vishnu) went into exile in the forest, a great deal of people accompanied him, but he told them that 'all the men and women can leave'. They did as instructed, returning from the outskirts of the forest to their homes in the kingdom.

When Rama returned from the forest many years later to reclaim his throne, it turned out that the hijras had gone on living at the edge of the forest, faithfully awaiting the return of their ruler. Moved by this act of devotion, Rama gave them the sacred power to bless and curse the 'regular' men and women, and promised them the attainment of Moksha ('spiritual liberation').[1]

Despite several centuries of British cultural and political occupation (with its Victorian priestly morality) leading hijras to be discriminated against in modern India, some Hindus still believe in their sacred powers.[2]

In the neighbouring countries of Nepal, Bhutan and Tibet, trans people were known as Pandaka (translated variously but taken to mean 'without defined gender').[3]

Let's return once more to ancient Ukraine – or Scythia, as it was known back then. The Scythians (and their close

---

1 Jeffrey Gettleman, 'The Peculiar Position of India's Third Gender', *New York Times* (17 February 2018).

2 ibid.

3 Richard Totman, 'Buddhism and the Third Gender' in *The Third Sex: Kathoey, Thailand's Ladyboys* (Chiang Mai: Silkworm Books, 2003).

YANA LYS

relations, the Sarmatians) shared the Greeks' belief in Amazons – gender-nonconforming women (some of whom are thought to have been transgender) – who formed a separate exclusive military 'caste'.[1] In ancient Greece, their name was popularly believed to be translated from 'breastless' – perhaps due to their self-identification and behaviour, which deviated from the social norms ascribed to women of the period. It was believed that the Amazons burned their chests and removed their breasts, in order that they might better use a bow. While modern scholarship does not find any evidence to support the rumours surrounding the removal of breasts, the fact that it so proliferated does point towards the possibility of transness.[2] Interestingly enough, in 2017 archaeologists found the grave of a Scythian woman warrior near the village of Hirnyts'ke in Dnipropetrovsk Oblast. She had been buried with a bow and a bunch of arrows.[3]

Generally speaking, unlike the Enarei, descriptions of the Amazons are more mythologised and vague, but they are much better known today. To this day, independent, militant women are referred to as Amazonians – but very few people know about the Enarei.

1 Herodotus, *Book IV: Melpomene, Histories*.
2 Natalie Haynes, 'The Amazons: Lives and Legends of Warrior Women Across the Ancient World', *Independent* (16 October 2014).
3 'Pod Dneprom nashli skhivskuyu amazonku' ('Scythian Amazon found near the Dnipro'), *Dnepr Vecherniy* (8 August 2017).

The Middle Ages

TRANSGENDER DEITIES OF UKRAINIAN

PAGANISM

The beginning of the Middle Ages saw the fall of the Roman Empire, and a great migration of people. Among many new European states, the Kievan Rus' appeared in the historical arena. Pagan until the tenth century, among the ancient Ukrainian polytheistic pantheon, Perun, Veles (Volos) and the goddess Makosh (Mokosh) held the highest esteem.

Interestingly, Christian apologetics (for example, in 'The Words of St Gregory' from the twelfth century) used an ancient Greek polysemantic word μαλακός (*malakos*) in their description of the proto-Slavic goddess Makosh, which was used to describe, amongst other things, effeminate men,[1] so it is not much of a stretch to think that, like Artimpasa, she was a deity of worship for trans people.

From time immemorial, on the saint's day of St Melania the Younger (the 13th of January, known as Malanka), during the festival, a boy was dressed up as a girl, called Melanka, and paraded about.[2] This custom still exists, and many ethnographers believe it to be an echo of the ancient worship

---

1 See also the Russian Bible Discussion Club article 'Kto takiye malakhy?' ('Who Are the Malakis?') for a contemporary discussion of the word in the context of its use in 1 Corinthians.
http://cogmtl.net/Qa/q043.htm

2 Oleksa Voropai, 'Zima' ('Winter') in *Zvichayi nashego narodu* (*Customs of Our People*) (Kyiv: Oberig, 1993).

of the goddesses Makosh and Veles, as the cross-dressing has nothing to do with the Christian tradition.[1]

This hypothesis of Makosh and Veles being deities of worship for transgender people in ancient times is supported by ethnographic evidence.

In the Galician village of Velesniv, for example, the name of which signifies past worship of Veles, there was a firmly held belief in a gender-transitioning tradition. Until as recently as the nineteenth century, it was believed that if someone were to go to the place from which the rainbow 'takes its water', the rainbow would drag the person along with it; after some time, it would release them back at the other end, but if the person was a boy, he would come out as a girl, and vice versa, and afterwards they would transition each month to a boy, then to a girl, and so on.[2]

This particular myth had slight variants in other areas. In some traditions, those who wanted to change their gender had set out while it was raining to go to the place from which the rainbow 'drinks water' and drink from the source themselves. Other interpretations of this myth advise people to 'simply' walk under the rainbow.[3]

A similar story from the same era in the Poltava Oblast had it that a boy born during the celebration of Malanka could transition to become a girl at will.[4]

---

1 Marta Patika, 'Stariy Noviy Rik. Svyato Vasylya ta Malanky' ('Old New Year: The Celebration of Vasyly and Malanka'), *Stozhary* (13 January 2014).

2 Valeriy Voytovych, *Anthology of Ukrainian Mythology* (Kyiv: Lybid, 2002).

3 ibid.

4 ibid.

So it certainly seems that in traditional Ukrainian culture trans people had some degree of visibility – otherwise where would all these ideas come from?

EARLY CHRISTIANITY AND TRANSNESS

The Age of Antiquity passed, and Christianity came, gaining a foothold on the territory of the Kievan Rus' in the tenth century. The Middle Ages and the politics of the Church are often blamed for sparking intolerant attitudes towards LGBTQI+ people and other minorities – but this isn't entirely correct.

In the Early Middle Ages (fifth–tenth centuries) and, to a certain extent, even in the High Middle Ages (eleventh–twelfth centuries), the Church was still relatively tolerant towards some forms of dissent. It was only in the Late Middle Ages (fourteenth–fifteenth centuries) that it became an agent of extremely authoritarian views.

Let's start by looking at the Gospel of Matthew. In it, the founder of Christianity talks about eunuchs, a word which, in the first-century Jewish communities, was not only the designation for castrated men, but also for intersex people – those born with sexual characteristics that cannot be purely defined as female or male: 'For there are eunuchs who were born that way, and there are eunuchs who have been made eunuchs by others – and there are those who choose to live like eunuchs for the sake of the Kingdom of Heaven. The one who can accept this should accept it.'[1]

---

1 Matthew 19:12 (NIV).

Christ's words here are in the context of his reflections on the masculinity and femininity, and there is not a trace of condemnation of eunuchs. He says, 'A man will leave his father and mother and be united to his wife, and the two will become one flesh... so they are no longer two, but one flesh.'[1]

In the apocryphal Gospel of Thomas, discovered by archaeologists, which scholars date (like the four canonical Gospels) to the first–second centuries, Jesus also states that people will enter the Kingdom of Heaven 'when you make the male and the female one and the same, so that the male not be male, nor the female...'[2]

Again, androgyny is presented here as the ideal state of being. The New Testament also mentions the baptism of a eunuch by Philip the Apostle.[3]

In the Middle Ages in Ukraine, until the sixteenth century, there existed an Orthodox ritual of huge importance: Adelphopoiesis, from the Greek for 'brother-making'.

The essence of Adelphopoiesis was the unification of two people of the same sex (most frequently men, who, predictably, enjoyed more liberties in the patriarchal Middle Ages) in a Church-sanctified union. This ritual was most widespread within the Greek and Slavic communities, and, from the tenth century, in the Kievan Rus'. The ceremony was outwardly very similar to the sacrament of marriage – both took place in front of the altar in a church.

Two men (or, in rare cases, women) who wanted to enter a brotherly (or sisterly) union stood in front of the Analogion,

---

1 Matthew 19:5–6 (NIV).

2 Thomas 22 (trans. Thomas O. Lambdin).

3 See Acts 8:27–39.

on which was laid a cross and the Gospel. The priest gave them candles to hold and joined their hands, after which he led them around the church, singing church songs, and gave them communion. The couple exchanged kisses with each other, kissed the priest and went on to the Agape feast.[1]

Among the Slavs Adelphopoiesis held the same importance as the sacrament of marriage. Indeed, people who entered such a brotherly union were considered to be related, and it could be an obstacle to marriage between members of their families. A partner in Adelphopoiesis had the right to inherit the property of his 'brother' in the event of his death.

It seems likely that the widespread uptake of Adelphopoiesis among the Slavs is explained by their pre-Christian traditions. 'Brotherly unions' also existed in Scythian culture, and were similarly enacted by special rituals. Wine was poured into a cup and mixed with the blood of the two, which they'd drink after taking an oath.[2]

Officially, Adelphopoiesis was perceived as a spiritual union, but we can be certain that gays, lesbians and trans people with an attraction to people of the same biological sex used Adelphopoiesis as an opportunity to legitimise their romantic relationships.

For a while, Adelphopoiesis was considered in a manner reminiscent of the 'don't ask, don't tell' approach, but a strengthening of authoritarian politics in the Church led to its outlawing on the grounds of it being 'unrighteous', and

---

1 John Boswell, *Same-Sex Unions in Pre-Modern Europe* (New York: Villard, 1994).

2 Herodotus, *Book IV: Melpomene, Histories*.

in Ukraine it was decisively outlawed under the reign of Metropolitan Petro Mohyla in the sixteenth century.

St Sergius and Bacchus, executed during the Roman Empire, are considered by many to be the founders of Adelphopoiesis.[1] According to their hagiography, after St Sergius and Bacchus refused to renounce the faith of Christ, they were dressed in women's clothes before they were tortured and executed. Was this simply a way of socially humiliating the warriors, based on the army code at the time, or was it perhaps an allusion to their self-identification? We don't have the historical data to answer this question – but it's a thought-provoking question indeed.

TRANSGENDER PEOPLE AND SKOROMOKHS

In the late Middle Ages, European societies experienced an ideological crisis. On one hand, the desire to revive the democratic and humanistic ideals of the Age of Antiquity was swiftly gaining steam; on the other, there was an increase in aspirations towards absolutism and authoritarianism from the rulers; and within the Church there was a push to conserve dogmatic belief and to opposite critical thought.

Unfortunately, humanism still had a long way to go. Europe was swept by religious wars, pogroms targeted Jews, witch hunts proliferated, along with not only the burning of books, but even the scientists who wrote them. Ukraine didn't remain untouched by these cruelties. Though not on the same scale as in western Europe, 'witches' were executed in

---

1 Boswell, *Same-Sex Unions in Pre-Modern Europe*.

Ukraine; all in all, approximately twenty thousand Ukrainian women were subjected to varying degrees of punishment following accusations of witchcraft.[1] It was made crystal clear to women that they were subordinate to men.

The creation myth of Adam and Eve was no longer related in a dualistic way – first there was an androgynous Adam, whom God split into two – but in a hierarchical way: first God created man, and then from just one part of his body (his rib) he created woman.[2]

In these conditions – the persecution of various minorities and the creation of a monolithic, God-fearing, obedient (to the Pope, bishops, kings, tsars, lords, etc.) majority of commoners – LGBTQI+ people, of course, came under persecution.

In Ukraine, for example, same-sex relationships were outlawed among the Zaporizhian Cossacks – offenders would be chained to the pillar of shame and beaten with sticks, sometimes to death. The existence of such a law, as noted by the historian Dmytro Yavornytsky, proves the existence of gays among the Cossacks.[3] Otherwise, why even introduce it?

---

1 Vakhtang Kipiani, 'Istoriya z vidmamy. Sudy pro chary v ukrainskich voyevodstvah Rechi Pospolitoyi XVII–XVIII stolitya' ('History with Witches: Witchcraft Trials in the Ukrainian Voivodeships of the Polish-Lithuanian Commonwealth of the 17th–18th Centuries'), *Istorychna Pravda* (10 June 2011).

https://www.istpravda.com.ua/reviews/2011/06/10/42247/

2 Nikolai Aleksandrovich Berdyaev, *The Meaning of the Creative Act*, trans. Donald A. Lowrie (New York: Gollancz, 1916).

3 Dmytro, Yavornytsky, 'Sudy, pokharannya i straty u zaporizkich kozakiv' ('Trials, Punishments and Executions Among the Zaporizhian Cossacks', The National Museum of History in Dnipro (no date).

http://www.museum.dp.ua/punishmentcossacks.html

Although it does needs to be highlighted that in the Zaporozhian Sich, which was perceived by Ukrainians as an Orthodox military knightly order, Cossacks were forbidden to have any sexual relations. Those who brought a woman into the Sich and engaged in sexual relations with her would be treated in exactly the exact same way as those committing the 'sin of Sodom'.

Transgender people, of course, were forced to lead a double life, like 'undercover agents', or risk their lives seeking to openly declare their identity. One of the few legal opportunities allowing transgender people to live openly in the Late Middle Ages was to join the travelling Skoromokhs, the so-called 'merry people', whom society permitted to cross-dress and perform their gender however they saw fit.

Interestingly, the Skoromokhs were regarded not simply as artists, but also as healers and soothsayers. Perhaps this was the last known sacralisation of transgender people on Ukrainian soil.

Skoromokhs are first mentioned in the letopises (chronicles) of Kievan Rus' in the eleventh century. At that time, their position was not only as travelling folk artists, but they were court artists as well. However, after only a few centuries, they were pushed to the margins. In the thirteenth century, the Metropolitan of Kievan Rus' Cyrill II called such acts 'devilish games', and they were essentially outlawed under the royal charter of 1648.[1]

---

1 Famyntsyn A. Skomorokhy, *Russkiy obraz zhizni* (*Russian Way of Life*) (Moscow: Institute of Russian Civilization, 2007), pp. 768–69. https://web.archive.org/web/20131029203057/http://www.rusinst.ru/docs/S_obraz.pdf

In the context of the transgender rainbow mythology (see p. 37), the word for 'rainbow' used is *veselka* – so perhaps the Skoromokhs, the '*veseli lyudy*' ('merry people'), could also be '*veselkovi*' ('rainbow people')?

Through the fifteenth and sixteenth centuries, Skoromokhs were targeted by both the Church authorities and those of secular beliefs. Language like 'God gave us a Pope, and the Devil gave us a Skoromokh' proliferated, and if they were caught, they faced execution. For their own safety, Skoromokhs gathered into large groups.

In the middle of the seventeenth century, with the help of Patriarch Nikon of Moscow, the Tsar officially prohibited Skoromokh performances, thus putting an end to the shows that tormented the Church.

Today the memory of these folk artists, who sheltered transgender people, is preserved in the names of villages in Lviv Oblast, Ternopil Oblast (in fact, there are two villages with this name in Ternopil Oblast), Ivano-Frankivsk Oblast, Zhytomyr Oblast, Vinnytsia Oblast and Cherkasy Oblast.[1]

Of course, even after losing this, the only semi-legal way of living openly in society, transgender people didn't disappear from Ukraine. Centuries of invisibility with little to no rights awaited them. However, there was hope ahead, when, in the Russian Empire's larger cities, groups of street actors (including trans and gender-nonconforming actors), re-emerged in the eighteenth century. And indeed, in Right Bank Ukraine and in Siberia, the last bands of Skoromokhs existed until the beginning of the nineteenth century.

---

1 Rostislav Pylypchuk, '*Skomorokh*', *About Ukraine: A Treasury of the Ukrainian People* (2017).
http://about-ukraine.com/skomorohi/

The New Age

MONASTICISM AND TRANSNESS

The Middle Ages passed, and the New Age began (from the sixteenth century to the beginning of the twentieth century). On one hand, in spite of the resistance from conservative post-medieval forces, it was a time of scientific development, belief in reason and the introduction of democratic ideas about the natural (innate) rights of every person to self-expression. However, in Ukraine, it was also a time of absorption by the Russian Empire, with its autocracy and serfdom.

The Constitution of Hetman Pylyp Orlyk (1710),[1] which was adopted earlier than the US Constitution (1787) became a purely declarative act. In essence, this unrealised Ukrainian Basic Law marked a peak in the development of Cossack freedoms and, simultaneously, their end – although the Sich existed until 1775, when it was destroyed by Russian empress Catherine II.[2] After this, the LGBTQI+ community in Ukraine was forced to retreat underground.

---

1 Ministry of Foreign Affairs of Ukraine, 'Constitution Day of Ukraine' (28 June 2016).
https://web.archive.org/web/20180419170120/https://mfa.gov.ua/en/news-feeds/foreign-offices-news/48775-deny-konstituciji-ukrajini

2 Yuriy Nikorak, 'Persha ukrainska konstituciya: 'batkyv' amerykanskoyi demokratiyi sche y na sviti ne bylo' ('The First Ukrainian Constitution: The 'Fathers' of American Democracy Did Not Even Exist'), *Ukrainian People: Ukrainian-American Magazine* (28 June 2017).
http://ukrainianpeople.us/перша-українська-конституція-батьк/

The only people who had a slight possibility of more or less legal self-expression were the nobility, so from now on we will focus on stories of the most famous transgender individuals, rather than the trans community as a whole.

Before zooming in, however, we must touch on the one semi-legal opportunity for some transgender people to realise themselves in society without facing direct condemnation which remained in the New Age. We are talking here about people who were assigned female at birth, who served in monasteries not as nuns, but as monks. There were a number of such cases, and the Church turned a blind eye to them. Sometimes, it even went beyond turning a blind eye – there are several Orthodox saints who fit this description!

First and foremost, Dosifey/a Kyivski/a, born Daryna Tyapkina (1721–76),[1] who was born into a noble family. When she was supposed to be married off, aged just sixteen, she fled from home, posing as a young man, Dosifey.[2]

Being a believer, he went to a monastery. Of course, this presented him with an opportunity to evade his family's search, and, for a brief time, he was a novice in the Trinity-Sergius Lavra near Moscow, but he never entered the monastic order, which involved the clipping of hair known as the tonsure, possibly fearing identification.

---

1 'Dosifey Kitaevsky', *The Orthodox Encyclopedia.*
https://www.pravenc.ru/text/180355.html

2 Dmitriy Butryn, 'Life in disguise', *Kommersant* (15 July 2016).
https://www.kommersant.ru/doc/3035923

Instead, he left the monastery and went to live in a cave in a desert just outside of Kyiv, where he lived as an ascetic hermit for seventeen years.[1] Due to his piousness, Dosifey quickly amassed a great respect amongst the people, and, in 1744, received a visit from none other than Empress Elizabeth (one of the only Russian monarchs with a liberal attitude towards Cossack liberation), the protection of whom allowed Dosifey to become a monk of the Kyiv-Pechersk Lavra. In 1776, shortly before his death, Dosifey gave his blessing to Prokhor Moshyn, the future great St Seraphim of Sarov, to receive his tonsure. In 1993, the Ukrainian Orthodox Church canonised Dosifey.

The Russians have a similar saint: Xeniya of St Petersburg, also known as Andrey the Fool.[2] After the death of her husband Andrey in the 1750s, Xeniya proclaimed that her husband Andrey Fyodorovich had not died, and she considered herself an incarnation of Andrey until her death.

Being noble-born, Xenia gave all her belongings away and led the life of pious asceticism, without formally accepting monasticism. In the end, St Petersburg residents grew accustomed to Andrey the Fool, and began to regard him as a visionary prophet. In 1988, the Russian Orthodox Church canonised him as Xeniya of St Petersburg.

---

1 'Zhitiye prepodobnoy Dosifei zatvornitsy Kyivskoy' ('Life of St Dosifeya, the Recluse of Kyiv'), Khram Svyatitelya Nikolaya Chudotvortsa na vodakh (Church of St Nicholas the Wonderworker on the Waters). http://hram-nikola.kiev.ua/
zhitiya-svyatykh/267-zhitie-prepodobnoj-dosifei-zatvornitsy-kievskoj
2 Xenia Cherkaev, 'St Xenia and the Gleaners of Leningrad', *The American Historical Review*, 125:3 (June 2020), pp. 906–14.

Of course, in Ukraine we're relatively familiar with the lives of saints, but there are similar instances of transgender monks who did not have the respect of the masses, and whose biographies are therefore completely unknown to us. It is worth noting that, in spite of the popularity and piety of these saints, Xeniya was only canonised during Gorbachev's Perestroika, and Dosifey was only made a saint in the early days of Ukraine's independence.

And of course, it won't have escaped your attention that both of these saints were born into nobility, which rather brings to mind a certain cinematic antihero's monologue that lambasts the 'average' middle-class viewpoint that regards someone from a lower-class background as crazy, while lauding the social elite as eccentric for the very same actions.

THE EVOLUTION OF THE CHURCH'S GENDER POLITICS

Of course, the modern Orthodox Church categorically denies the transgender identities of these saints, and instead says they simply had a special spiritual journey – that they escaped from 'worldly life', using foolishness (insanity) 'for the sake of Christ', in order to go beyond the social norms of the secular world that lives in sin.

However, here's what's particularly interesting: we're unable to find a single case of this working in the opposite direction – that is to say, for example, there are no recorded cases of transgender people assigned male at birth taking holy orders as a nun to avoid marriage, say, or to avoid serving in the army in an aggressive, thereby sinful, war. Neither are there any records of people assigned male at birth presenting as female in the public sphere. What's more, when joining her order, a nun could take on the name of a male saint, even if she was only a novice and did not present as a man, because monkship is an angelic rank, and angels have no gender.

Why could this be? Surely only because the ideology of patriarchal chauvinism prevailed during the High Middle Ages. A woman, as noted above, began to be perceived as an extension of man, derived from his flesh – and of course also as the original sinner, tempting man with the forbidden fruit from the tree of knowledge.

Historical evidence suggests that, in the Early Middle Ages, women were ordained not only as deaconesses, but as priests (presbyterids),[1] but this was obscured from the historical record. Rumours abound that St Brigit of Ireland was even ordained a bishop in the sixth century,[2] but likewise this is categorically denied, and all such tales are lumped together as early medieval perversions of the Church, steering it from its rightful path.

It seems if a woman wanted to become a 'higher' being, a man – although not in the sense of gaining equality in terms of power within the Church, but in the context of religious asceticism – it was sometimes permitted, if condescendingly. On the other hand, if a man were to attempt the reverse, the patriarchal society could only regard this as a desire to move

---

1 Dmitry Zenchenko, 'O meste zhenshchiny v pastyrskom sluzhenii' ('On the Place of Women in Pastoral Ministry') *Christianity for All* (30 July 2008).

2 talifa88, 'Svyataya Brigitta – yepiskopessa Drevney Irlandii' ('Saint Brigid – Bishop of Ancient Ireland'), *Livejournal* (2013).

from a 'higher' state to a lower, more sinful one. Where's any kind of spiritual feat in that? It's a fall from grace, and that's all that could be said about it. But either way, after the eighteenth century, the social tolerance for women who sought to realise themselves as spiritual male ascetics had all but vanished.

Once again broadening this to a pan-Indo-European cultural context, let us recall the fate of the world-famous French national heroine, Joan of Arc.

When in 1431 the English – with the Church's support – burned Joan at the stake, she was condemned not only for 'heresy' or 'witchcraft', but also for wearing men's clothing. In other words, according to the cultural standards of medieval Europe, she was condemned for her gender nonconformity.

During the Middle Ages, wearing trousers, a fashion brought to Europe by Scythian men, was strictly forbidden for women. Worse yet was Joan's decision to wear a knight's armour in battle.

After almost five hundred years passed, European women finally obtained the right to wear men's clothing. At first this was taken up only by the aristocracy, intelligentsia and bohemians, then later by the progressive bourgeoisie, but with the passage of time, it permeated all layers of society.

Of course, under pressure from the French, who defeated the English and defended their sovereignty, the Church posthumously removed the charge of heresy from Joan of Arc in 1456, and eventually, in 1920, Joan was canonised as a Catholic saint.

So here is laid stark the evolution of so-called 'eternal' religious values, seemingly independent of the political and cultural landscape of its community across the historical era.